STATION ZARAHEMLA

A Short Story

By

STEVEN HEUMANN

Printed in the United States of America

First Printing, 2019

ISBN 9781082423833

www.stevenheumann.com

STATION ZARAHEMLA
Judge's Log: 473-119

"I want them executed yesterday!" Pacumení screamed, slamming his hand against the velvet-wrapped armrest of his Chief Judge throne. Red and gold ceremonial robes swished back and forth as the man's arms waved wildly like a toddler in a tantrum.

Helaman took a calming breath, allowing the filtered air from the station's climate processors to fill his lungs with a sanitized mixture of oxygen and nitrogen. Kept at an uncomfortably cold temperature, the Judgement Hall seemed designed to intimidate and unbalance with its grandeur. Shiny metal pillars reached four stories up to the arched ceiling above, creating a cavernous space that Helaman always detested in its self-important opulence.

His agitated foot tapped the burnished tiles, producing a light thumping sound with the boot's rubber soles. He watched Pacumení's reflection in the glass behind the judge as it mirrored his silly movements against a field of emotionless stars. His own reflection looked back at him, along with the faces of the three council men in their gray and yellow uniforms.

"With all due respect, Chief Judge," Helaman said, hands held dutifully behind his back. "The conspirators fled before we even knew Pahoran had been murdered. All of the cameras had been deactivated from here to the hangar bay where their ship was docked. We have trackers on their trail, but we need time. This can't be rushed, otherwise we'll end up condemning innocent people just so we can feel like we've done something."

"We have several suspects," Councilman Antiom added, sweat glistening on his forehead.

"I don't care!" Pacumení bellowed from his raised dais, voice echoing off the high ceilings and shiny metal surfaces of the Magistrate Hall. Pointing toward the Chief Judge throne, he continued. "Yesterday as I sat on this very seat I looked down and saw my brother's blood dried in one of the crevices. Even after being cleaned three times, I still found Pahoran's gore as a reminder that he was murdered on this very throne; holding this very office!" He tugged on his ceremonial robes in emphasis.

Helaman took a step forward, hands moving outward in a calming motion. "Pacumení, if you're going to occupy that seat, you're going to need to take a breath. The people were nervous after the trial and execution of Paanchi, and that was before your predecessor was murdered in political retaliation."

"I don't need advice from you, Helaman," Pacumení said, sitting down in his elevated seat. "If I want religious guidance, I'll go to you."

The gathered delegates murmured quietly at the Chief Judge's flippant comment. Helaman's neck tightened, muscles straining against his dark blue uniform.

"I may be the High Priest of our religion, but I'm also a judge just like you were before the election," Helaman informed.

"I don't need political lessons right now," Pacumení said with a dismissive wave. "What I need is for the climate techs to fix the air conditioning in my office, so it isn't so cold in here, and for all of you to bring me news that you've captured the man who murdered our previous Chief Judge. This meeting is over."

"Yes, your honor," two of the councilmen chorused, looking to Antiom as if asking permission to leave.

"Thank you, oh wise judge Pacumení," Antiom said with a bow before backing away and motioning for his colleagues to follow.

Helaman rolled his eyes and turned toward the ornate wooden doors leading to the main hallway. "You don't have to bow to him, Antiom," he said as they reached the exit. "He's not our king. We elected him just as we did his father and brother before him."

"I like to show proper respect for our elevated leader," Antiom replied.

The decorative doors slid open, allowing a wave of warmer air to blow through Helaman's short black hair and send goosebumps up his arms. A crush of conversation rode the breeze as the voices of thousands of people echoed from the central ring plaza less than 500 feet to the left. Smells of roasted meat and fried vegetables met Helaman's nose, causing his stomach to grumble in neglect.

High ceilings ten-stories tall ran along the entire center of the station's outer ring. Shops, restaurants, small trees, and movie theaters lined the edges of the unending plaza, disappearing in the distance as the ground slowly sloped into an eternal circle spinning in space. Only here where the open expanse continued without obstruction could residents see the curvature of the ring from the inside and appreciate Zarahemla's true scale.

"Don't be such a sycophant, Antiom," Helaman said, turning to the left away from the central plaza. "Pahoran the First was a great leader, but his sons didn't exactly follow in his footsteps; Pacumení included."

"That is our elected leader you're talking about," Antiom

said with an exaggerated shiver, as if Helaman's words offended him so much he couldn't control his own body. His colleagues on the Station Council remained silent behind him. Their eyes shifted back and forth as if unsure whether they should support their fellow councilman's statement or not.

"You're right," Helaman conceded. "But that doesn't mean we bow to him and accept everything he says as gospel."

Antiom stepped in front of Helaman, face stern and self-important. "What does the rest of your afternoon look like, Helaman? We must discover where the conspirators fled. I have several investigators coming to my office with their progress on the assassination inquiry. You will accompany me to the council chambers where members of the media will be asking questions regarding our advancements."

"I appreciate your enthusiasm, Antiom. I truly do," Helaman said, placing his hand firmly on the councilman's shoulder. "But at this point I need to see my family and talk to Captain Moronihah. He messaged me last week that some of the border stations had picked up strange enemy activity. I want to know what his intelligence officers have discovered. After that I have a meeting with some of the clergy that I will be attending."

"May I remind you that your status as a lower judge is more important than your duties as a religious leader?" Antiom said, words dripping with condescension.

Helaman smiled, biting his tongue. "May I remind *you* that I outrank you, and that I like to concentrate more on actual work than on how the media perceives me. If we're going to keep this station from falling into chaos, I need to be doing all my jobs, civil and religious. I'm not answering the exact same questions the reporters asked last week just so I can look good to everyone. I'll leave that to you."

Lips pressed together in frustration, Antiom nodded. "Very well, but I want to know what Moronihah has to say immediately after you've spoken to him."

Helaman turned and waved over his shoulder at the councilman. "You'll get my report along with everyone else on the council. Good day, gentlemen."

As he walked down the main hall, minor vibrations rippled up Helaman's legs from the floor. The hairs on his arms lifted somewhat, as if the air pressure had lightened. Gravity along the center ring always fluctuated between slightly too strong and too weak. Each rotation of the enormous loop had to be counter-balanced against the additional sections that had been added to the station over the past 50 years. As a child Helaman remembered running down this hall with his friends completely unaware of air currents and gravity. Now as the station had grown it seemed every system became taxed to the breaking point. Even the water tasted funny, as if the filters couldn't remove all the oil and waste that accumulated in the pipes.

He waved to a group of passing soldiers on their way to the holographic training center on the lower levels. Their boots smacked against the floor in unison, reminding Helaman of his cadet days during the Lamanist War. He never again wanted to experience the horrors of battle but knew the current climate of unrest and unease pushed them closer to conflict both at home and abroad.

"Judge Helaman!" a woman shouted behind him. "Judge Helaman! I have those documents for you to sign."

Helaman turned to see his young law clerk Ruth running up to him with a clear holo-pad in her hand. Red hair bounced against her shoulders, a fitting illustration of her boundless energy.

"Ruth," Helaman said, trying not to chuckle as she skidded up to him and almost tripped over her own feet. "I don't need to sign those until tomorrow. You didn't need to track me down."

Panting from her jog, Ruth shook her head. "Judge Leah asked me if you could get them to her by the end of the day and I said yes, so here I am."

"Alright, I'll sign them." Helaman took the holo-pad and scrolled through the documents, signing his finger across each one. "Hey, Ruth, since you're here, you wouldn't happen to have your signal booster with you by chance? I need to contact Captain Moronihah, and mine's back at the office."

"I do," the young woman said, reaching over to the computer on her left wrist and popping a clear marble from one of the receivers. "I always have it with me in case Jonathan tries to call from the border fleet. We talked earlier today though, so you can use it if you need."

"Your boyfriend is a lucky man, and so am I. I'll have this back to you tomorrow morning. That alright?"

"For sure," Ruth chirped, turning on her heals to head back the way she came. "I'll get these to Judge Leah and finalize the docket for tomorrow."

"Thank you, as always Ruth."

She bounded off, practically skipping while humming a popular tune slightly off pitch.

Tapping his wrist computer, Helaman waited for the flashing blue screen to respond before placing the small sphere in the amplifier.

"Judge Helaman," the synthetic voice stated, waves of color dancing along the glass with each word. "How may I help you this afternoon?"

"I need to see if Captain Moronihah is in sync for a live call."

"Signal augmentation crystal accepted. Contacting Captain Moronihah."

"They're all dead, sir," Lieutenant Jesse said, motioning toward the damaged central console of the command deck.

Evidence of fires scarred the chairs and walls, long since extinguished by a lack of oxygen. Only eight bodies littered the floor, meaning most of the administration crew had escaped to other sections of the space station prior the slaughter.

Moronihah rubbed his finger along the soot sticking to what once had been a polished glass control panel. "Have we reestablished atmosphere throughout the station?" he asked, scratching his dark beard.

"Only to the command center and outer ring, sir," the lieutenant answered. "The interior additions are still cut off from the vents. That's probably where the last survivors holed-up during the attack. Gideon Station is a total loss."

Looking around the executive bridge, Moronihah took in every detail. Cracks along the protective windows evidenced laser burns; some sort of attack happened on the bridge prior to the atmosphere failing. Two of the dead crewmen still clung to their plasma pistols, showing they had put up a fight. The smell of smoke lingered, as did the rotten fragrance of decomposing corpses. The atmospheric processors may have been shut off to asphyxiate everyone onboard, but the oxygen hadn't been jettisoned into space, allowing putrefaction to progress. Even in the haptic-sealed bridge, bacteria began to spoil the bodies.

During peak hours the command center would have bustled with at least 20 officers and crew. Station Gideon had been small; only 30 thousand people. Now after what had obviously been a brutal attack, the population had dropped to zero.

Men, women, children; none had been spared when the

invading force descended and eventually choked off the central atmosphere processors.

An image of his teenage daughter Naomi arguing with him back home on Station Noah about staying out too late with local boys came to Moronihah's mind. As angry as she made him, he felt the sudden urge to call her and make sure she was alright.

"Please tell me there are survivors somewhere on this station," Moronihah said.

"No life signs, sir."

The urge to smash his fists against the control panels almost overthrew Moronihah's professional façade.

30 thousand people. All dead.

One way or another this would lead to war. Millions more would likely perish in fire because of this attack.

"Why wouldn't they have taken over the station like they used to?" Jesse asked. "Turn it into a Lamanist base?"

Moronihah looked down at the frozen eyes of one of the command crew bodies. "I'm not sure. This is beyond a mere military strike. Most of this base was made up of civilians. Do we know whose force attacked yet?"

"Reports are saying Coriantumr, sir. Several station ships escaped during the attack, and they are reporting the main flagship was adorned with the red circle of Crimson Descent."

"Where is her fleet heading? Any signs?"

Jesse kneeled next to one of the corpses and pulled on the sleeve to check for a rank. "None, sir. The body of Governor Jerusalem should be here on the command deck, but none of these bodies look to be him. He wouldn't have fled, do you think?"

"No," Moronihah said with a shake of the head. "Jerusalem will be on this station somewhere. He would have fought to the last."

"What do we do about Coriantumr?"

Moronihah motioned for one of the soldiers guarding the entrance to step over. "We wait and see. Officer: send word to the rest of the unit that we will be leaving within the hour. Understood? I need to get word to Pacumení and Helaman immediately."

"Yes, sir," the soldier replied.

"Do you think Coriantumr will head to station Teancum next?" Jesse asked, standing back up and dusting his hands against his red and gold uniform. "It's only slightly bigger than Gideon. It would be an easy target if they caught it off-guard."

"We haven't received any reports of activity in that quadrant. I'm not sure what Coriantumr is thinking right now. It's been ten years since the war ended and I don't think the Lamanist government is any keener to start a new one than the judges at Zarahemla."

A soldier dressed in blue and yellow ceremonial robes stepped onto the bridge, hands folded in front of her. "Captain Moronihah," she said, eyes forward, back ridged. "The communication team has received a message request from Zarahemla, sir."

"Who is it?" Moronihah asked.

"Helaman, the son of Helaman, sir."

"Excellent. Patch him through directly to me."

The soldier handed Moronihah a crystal marble, bowed quickly and ushered herself out. Moronihah placed the small sphere into the receiver on his wrist communicator and waited for the ball to change color. It flashed blue, verifying a strong signal strength for live trans-space communication.

"Helaman?" Moronihah said, tapping the marble to verify the two men were connected. "Helaman, are you receiving?"

"Moronihah," Helaman's voice replied, echoing in the quiet command bridge. "Can you hear me?"

"I can, and it's a good signal. It's wonderful to hear from you, my friend."

"And you, Moronihah. How are things along the border?"

The captain paced from one end of the bridge to the other, stepping over bodies as he thought of the best way to report their findings. "Bad. Station Gideon has been attacked."

"Are the Lamanists occupying the station?" Helaman asked.

"No. They destroyed the atmospheric filters and asphyxiated everyone onboard and moved on. I'm here right now standing amidst the bodies."

"Everyone is dead? How many people lived on Gideon? It had to be tens of thousands."

"Just shy of thirty thousand."

"Thirty thousand? They killed thirty thousand people? That's an act of war not seen since the destruction of Ammonihah Station. Why would they do that?! During the war it was all about capturing outposts and using them to gain more spatial territory."

Moronihah nodded to the voice as if the two men sat in the same room. "I know. It's a travesty. I'm not sure what they're planning, but we have evidence Coriantumr is in command of the fleet."

Taking a deep breath on the other side of the signal, Helaman spat in anger. "Thirty thousand people! I'm going to call the Council of Judges as soon as I'm done talking to you. Get us your report fast. Have they hit any other stations on the border?"

"No. I'm not sure what they're planning. We need to be vigilant and on high alert. How are things on the capitol?"

"That's why I wanted to contact you, actually. Have you heard any more rumors of who led the team that broke into the Judgement Hall and assassinated Pahoran?"

"Only whispers," Moronihah replied. "But I may have a

name for you. Kishkumen."

"I've heard of that guy before, I think. Didn't he work for the Morianton Crime Family and got caught up in that sting operation a few years ago?"

"The same. It's all I have though; nothing more than a rumor. Everyone has been surprisingly tight-lipped about this whole thing."

"I appreciate the info all the same," Helaman said. "I'll pass the name along to the head investigator and then press some of my contacts in the courts to see what I come up with."

"How is Pacumení?" Moronihah asked, tripping on the leg of one of the bodies at his feet. "I may not have voted for him, but I hope he's well, all the same."

"He's paranoid, but that's to be expected after your predecessor, who also happened to be your brother, is assassinated while holding your same office. Hopefully, he'll follow in his father's footsteps, given enough time. He has a lot to live up to if you ask me."

"The same can be said of both of us," Moronihah supposed.

"Too true. It's the burden of having famous dads, I guess."

"And your grandfather was even chief judge, for pity's sake. Legacy takes its toll."

"Thanks for your time, Moronihah," Helaman said. "Keep me informed if anything on the border changes. I'm afraid we're on the verge of war again after only a decade of peace. It's not enough time."

"It never is, Helaman. I'll talk to you soon."

"Thanks, Moronihah."

The marble blinked red, signaling the report's termination. Moronihah turned toward the door and waved for Lieutenant Jesse to follow him off the bridge.

"Get the clean-up crew in here as soon as you can get a report out," he said, walking with determined strides. "Also, send word to every ship in the fleet to have their sensors searching for any movement along border space. If Coriantumr is looking to fight, we better be ready. Put every space station along the frontier on alert as well. I don't want another base falling prey to the Lamanist armada."

"Yes, sir," Jesse answered with a nod.

"Thirty thousand people, all dead."

Helaman sat next to his wife on the couch, taking a sip from the freshly squeezed grape juice she had bought for him. He snuggled close to Isabel, content to be home after a long day of dealing with lower judge burdens mixed with the duties of High Priest. Stars smiled down on the couple through the glass partitions on the ceiling, reminding Helaman of the bigger universe beyond his daily grind inside the Zarahemla political machine. Through the window he could see the far side of the station ring twenty miles away; lights flickering in the distance like winking eyes.

"Do you think we're going to war again?" Isabel asked, running her fingers through her long black hair. She pulled her bare feet up next to her on the couch, as if contracting against the thought of bloody conflict.

"I talked to six of the lead judges but couldn't get in direct contact with Pacumení because of his speaking engagement at the Joseph Memorial Library," Helaman said, squeezing his wife harder than intended. "We're going to meet first thing in the morning and then make a public statement."

"I don't want our boys fighting in a war like you had to." Isabel glanced over at a collection of blankets hanging from chairs across the room. "Nephi's only 15 years old. Lehi would die if his older brother had to go fight in battles on the other side of the galaxy. They built that fort together this afternoon and played in it with their sisters. I don't even want to think about what happens if we declare war."

Glancing at the family photos along the walls, a pang of regret filled Helaman's chest. Zarahemla had been his home since childhood, but more and more he wished to take his own children away from the congested, politically charged station of over twelve million people. As a judge, and the son of a beloved military and religious leader, life had been anything but quiet and enjoyable over the past decade. Would things have been better if the family had moved to Lebanon after the war, or maybe Bountiful Station at the very least?

If they had left years before, would they now be embroiled in a potentially devastating war?

"We're not going to DEFCON-1," Helaman stated, taking another drink of the richly flavored liquid. "Since the assassination, everyone is on edge. We'll figure something out. Plus, Nephi wouldn't have to fight if he didn't want to. Our military is strong; we won't be drafting 15-year-olds any time soon. Don't worry about it."

Isabel smiled, running her fingers through Helaman's dark hair. "I'll do my best. You'll be building up some vacation time so we can take the kids to the lake on Lebanon, right? They need to get off this station and breathe some unfiltered air for a change. Get bitten by some insects or something. It will be good for them."

"I'm still planning on the trip to Lebanon over the summer season, don't worry. The kids will swim in real fresh water before they get too old."

"Speaking of getting too old," Isabel said, taking the glass from Helaman's hand and drinking the last sip of juice before he had a chance to. "You need to take Nephi for his pilot test."

"I don't want to talk about this," Helaman said.

"He's 15 now. You can't keep avoiding this forever."

Helaman laid his head back against the couch. "I just remember my first piloting lesson with my dad. It didn't go well."

"Oh, I've heard the stories from your uncle Shiblon," Isabel laughed. "They were very detailed. Just because you crashed in the landing bay and got all embarrassed in front of Captain Moroni doesn't mean Nephi will. He's more thoughtful than you, anyway. He'll do great."

"I know he will," Helaman admitted, grabbing the glass from his wife, and tipping it back over his mouth to see if even a single drop of juice had escaped Isabel's thirst. "I just have to admit he's growing up, which is the harder thing for me to---"

A tremor ran from the floors, up the walls, and shook the entire quarters. Helaman squeezed the couch arm involuntarily in surprise.

"What was that?" Isabel asked, sitting up straight.

Helaman shot to his feet. "I don't know."

"Is the gravity on the fritz again? Last time we were in semi-weightlessness for three hours on this sector."

"I don't think it---"

The station shook a second time, more violently than the first. One of the blanket-covered chairs fell over and thumped against the carpet. Helaman stomped toward the door, thankful he hadn't yet taken his boots off.

"Stay here with the kids," he said, pointing at his wife. "I need to head to the Judge's Chambers. Prepare to detach the escape pod if I send you the signal at any point."

"What's going on?" Isabel asked, fear creeping into her voice.

"I think we're under attack!"

Before he finished the sentence, flashes of light filled the room through the glass ceiling as explosions detonated against the station's hull on the other side of the ring.

"Who's attacking Zarahemla?!" Isabel shouted as she stumbled over to the table.

"Just keep the kids safe and be ready to jettison if we have to!" Helaman charged from the room and headed toward the front door.

Shouts filled the hallway as he exited; people scrambling out their doors in pajamas and slippers while vibrations continued to rumble through the station. All the way down the hall dozens of doors slid open; hundreds of people clogging the corridor with confused expressions and half-awake eyes.

"Judge Helaman! Are we under attack?" one of his neighbors, an old man named Omner, asked while holding firmly to his cane.

An alarm sounded, filling the hallway with the grating sound of artificial squealing. Emergency lights flared red, strobing in systematic rhythm with the alert.

Helaman pointed toward the doors along the hallway's left side as he pushed past a scared young woman holding a crying toddler in her arms. "Everyone, stay in your homes! If we *are* under attack, the Watch Defense will repel the invaders with their strike ships. Get back inside for now!"

While the words made sense and acted as a check on the fear in the civilian's eyes, Helaman knew the Watch would be insufficient against a full assault. Most of the army had been stationed along the border with Moronihah. Perimeter sensors over a lightyear from Zarahemla would have sent advanced warning of any assault and given battle cruisers enough time to respond. The thought of a fleet of ships sneaking past and descending directly on the capital seemed farfetched at best.

Unlikely or not, that possibility had now become a reality as another blast rocked Zarahemla, throwing Helaman into an obese man wearing nothing but a bathrobe.

Helaman pushed himself off the large gentleman and tapped frantically at his wrist computer. Colors swirled on the screen forming a purple warning symbol.

"All broadcast channels are temporarily backlogged with calls," the pleasant computer voice chirped. "Please wait for a channel to become available before attempting another call. Thank you."

"Come on!" Helaman shouted. "As soon as a line opens send a message to Moronihah that Zarahemla is under attack! Use priority code Helaman 5-12."

"All broadcast channels are temporarily backlogged with calls," the computer repeated.

"Just send the message when one opens up!"

Running at full speed, he headed for the Judgement Hall. As he passed a series of extended windows, Helaman caught a glimpse of the scale of the attack. Hands pressing against the glass, he watched as the entire Lamanist fleet converged on the station, firing cannons and tachyon blasters indiscriminately.

Over two hundred spacecraft darted between the columns extending from the station hub to the outer ring. Some vessels were nothing more than small individual fighters while others filled Helaman's view and disappeared behind sections of the space station. The largest battle cruiser Helaman estimated had to be at least five miles from bow to stern with three engines on each side of its oval hull. Weapons discharged in all directions with thoughtless abandon. Cruisers swirled like locusts on a breeze, converging on Watch Defense ships and obliterating the defenders without hesitation.

Explosions lit up the darkness of space for a fraction of a second before dissipating in the void. Flashes of cobalt streaked like lightening and blew chunks of metal from Zarahemla's hull. Debris pelted the reinforced glass and ricocheted into the vacuum on a never-ending journey through the stars.

How had an enemy armada gotten past the deep space perimeter sensors?

Several troop transport ships descended on Zarahemla's exterior like gigantic metal spiders; enormous steel claws penetrating the station's thick protective shielding to allow the Lamanist army access to the inside of the base.

Everything from the ferocity of the attack to the sheer speed with which the invaders swooped in, left Helaman at a loss for how to repel the assault.

Screams continued to cascade down the hallway from living quarters on all sides, reminding Helaman what Moronihah had told him about Gideon Station and the massacre there. Would Zarahemla be next?

Helaman pulled himself from his front row seat and continued toward the Judgement Hall. He turned the corner and charged toward the central plaza, shouting for civilians to go back into their homes. A group of soldiers shuffled from a side corridor and almost knocked him over. Several of the troopers fumbled to put on their boots while others checked their weapons to verify ammo levels.

"Sorry, sir!" one of the soldiers, a tall, gangly young man no older than 20, shouted over the alarm. "Are you Judge Helaman? You came to my church once and spoke on the power of faith."

"I am. What unit are you?" Helaman asked as the entire station seemed to shudder under the onslaught.

"We're about half of the S.W. 457, sir," the thin soldier stated, pimpled face accenting his youth.

"Who's the ranking officer?"

"I am," the soldier answered hesitantly. "Our C.O. hasn't come back to the barracks yet. We don't know where he is. We're all on leave from the fleet. I'm just a corporal."

"You'll do. Come with me," Helaman ordered, pointing toward the rounded main hallway entrance less than two hundred feet away. "We're going to the Judgement Hall to make sure Pacumení is safe."

"Yes sir!" the officer said with a quick salute.

Followed by 12 soldiers in various conditions of undress, Helaman ran into the station's central corridor. Luckily the plaza appeared all but deserted this late at night, with only a handful of teenagers bolting past chairs and tables in a food court before charging into a shoe store, waved in by an elderly man wearing a chef's smock.

"Keep running!" Helaman pushed, making sure none of the soldiers fell behind. "How many of you are armed?"

"Only eight of us, sir," the corporal answered.

"What's your name?"

"Samuel, sir."

"Well, Corporal Samuel," Helaman said as they barged past the reception area next to the Judgment Hall entrance. "Get your people ready to help protect the Chief Judge."

Slamming his shoulder against the heavy wooden doors, Helaman forced the barrier open and stepped into the gallery. Rifles clicked in response to their hasty entrance.

"Helaman?" Pacumení yelled from behind a cadre of twenty guards dressed in full red and gold armor complete with helmets and ceremonial capes. "What's happening out there? Ships are flying by the windows and firing on the hull. Lamanist ships! Where's Moronihah with my army?"

"Along the celestial border," Helaman said, stepping between the guards toward Pacumení. Spacecraft zoomed past the observation glass, exploding in fleeting sparks as other ships fired from somewhere above. Wreckage pelted the armor-plated window, tinging like stones against corrugated metal. "The entire Lamanist fleet is here."

Pacumení stumbled back, tripping on the steps leading up to his Judgment Seat. "What?! The full fleet? Here in the heart of our territory? How did they get past our armies? The Perimeter Sentries?"

Helaman grabbed Pacumení by his robes and pulled the judge toward the far door. "I don't know, but we need to get you to safety. We should head toward the station center where the shielding is the strongest."

"Okay, that's a good plan," Pacumení agreed. "Men, let's follow Judge Helaman---"

The main doors exploded sending shavings of fine wood tumbling through the air. Chunks smacked Helaman's face, cutting his cheeks with tiny slivers.

"Protect the Chief Judge!" one of the soldiers shouted as weapons fire filled the Judgement Hall.

Laser blasts of red and orange striated the room leaving smoking craters in their wake. Tile and concrete exploded in ear-splitting pops, sending pieces of masonry tumbling into the air. The soldier next to Helaman took a high-intensity discharge to the chest and fell without a cry. Pacumení's guards returned fire as Lamanist soldiers in black and yellow armor scurried through the smoke-filled entrance.

"We need to get out of here!" Helaman shouted to Corporal Samuel as the young fighter emptied his pistol toward the advancing legion.

"Get me to the panic room in the back!" Pacumení cried over

the deafening pound of rifles and plasma cannons.

Blood sprayed against Helaman's boots in tiny droplets as another Zarahemla soldier fell at his feet.

"Grenade!" someone yelled.

Before Helaman could turn in the direction of the shout, fire singed his face as the incendiary ignited in a thunderous bang. Feet left the floor as Helaman felt himself flying backward through the air. He hit the tile hard, smacking the back of his head on impact and rolling to his side. Stars danced in front of his eyes, a throbbing pain coursing from his neck to his stomach. Smoke and flame filled Helaman's lungs, forcing a cough from deep in his chest.

Shouts and weapons fire continued echoing around him, but they seemed distant and muffled. Ears ringing, Helaman tried to push himself up when another explosion pounded against his body and skidded him five feet across the smooth inlay. A warm wetness soaked his dark blue judge's uniform below his left ribs. Pain shrieked like a screaming child at two in the morning. He reached his right hand over to feel a jagged piece of shrapnel about two inches long embedded in his flesh.

Helaman blinked trying to wash away the blur that impeded his vision. Everything seemed to move in slow motion. Several Zarahemla soldiers fell in hails of gunfire. The Judgement Seat smoked like a green stalk as flames consumed the velvety armrests and cushion.

"Sir! Get up!" Corporal Samuel shouted, tugging on Helaman's arm to help the judge to stand. "We have to retreat!"

Focusing on the young man's face, Helaman regained control of his senses. "Where's Pacumení?"

"Sir, we need to---" A laser blast hit Samuel in the neck, choking off his words.

"Samuel!" Helaman cried, grabbing the corporal as the man fell back, blood spurting from his mouth. The cauterized neck wound told Helaman everything he needed to know: the soldier wouldn't survive more than a few minutes. He pulled the boy toward the windows and away from the battle, laying him down on the dusty tile behind one of the pillars. Shock and pain registered in Samuel's eyes as his throat spasmed. Body tensing and then going limp, the lieutenant died without a whimper.

"Helaman! Get me out of here!" Pacumení screamed from behind his burning Judgement Seat.

Only three Zarahemla soldiers remained alive, guns blazing in one final push to save the Chief Judge. Two dozen Lamanist soldiers charged into the hall and cut down the stoic defenders, leaving only Helaman and Pacumení breathing. Silence fell, interrupted by pieces of debris smacking against the glass from the space battle outside, and the crackle of flames still chewing on the Judgement Seat upholstery.

"Drop your weapons!" one of the invaders shouted with a thick Lamanist accent, jumping around the pillar, and pointing his rifle at Helaman.

"I'm unarmed," Helaman informed, raising his hands in surrender.

"I don't have any guns!" Pacumení cried, still crouched behind the chair.

"Bring the judge here!" a Lamanist commander in a gray and yellow uniform ordered. Tattoos of spiked thorns around the man's eyes betrayed his status as a Lamanist Shock General; trained in brutal guerrilla warfare and destabilization. Helaman had encountered many such leaders during the war; and many of their victims.

Three soldiers pushed Helaman forward while two others pulled on Pacumení and forced him down the stone steps toward the conquering legion.

"You have no right to be here!" Pacumení shrieked, clinging

to the hems of his robes to keep from tripping on the fabric. "This is an act of war!"

The Shock General raised his fist to backhand the judge when a shout gave the sinister man pause.

"Stop, General Cohor," a feminine voice commanded. "We must treat the Chief Judge with the utmost respect."

The words, each perfectly pronounced with a Zarahemla inflection, reminded Helaman of something an attorney would say as opposed to an invading general.

"Coriantumr?" Pacumení spat, pushing against the guards holding him in place. "What is the meaning of this?! You have no right to come here and attack this station!"

Coriantumr stepped out from behind her personal guard and grinned; perfect white teeth shining in the light of the dying fires. In her mid-forties, the commander still held onto the beauty of her youth, but her dark eyes betrayed the ambition and cruelty that had made her infamous throughout the space ways. Her hair, short on the sides and pulled up into a tall pompadour, came to a widow's peak on the center of her forehead where a large red circle had been tattooed, marking her as the leader of the Crimson Descent.

"Ah, Pacumení," she said, sauntering up to the two judges while stepping over a dead body with a smoking chest wound. "It's been too long since we debated the merits of democracy verses monarchy. You've done quite well for yourself since I defected to the Lamanists, I see."

"I demand you remove your forces from this station immediately!" Pacumení yelled; spittle dribbling down his lip.

Helaman stood straight and tall, focusing past the pain in the back of his head and under his left arm.

"How did you get here so quickly?" he asked, coughing on the thick vapor hanging in the air. "How did you know we would be here in the Judgement Hall?"

Stepping close to Helaman, Coriantumr looked the judge up and down with the scrutiny of an art dealer appraising a painting.

"High Priest Helaman. It's good to finally meet you. Honestly, I didn't know *you* would be here, but my informants told me exactly where *he* would be." She pointed at Pacumení. "I knew if this whole thing was going to work it would need to be quick, so as soon as we arrived at Zarahemla my personal dropship descended with my best legion to procure the Chief Judge."

"You will not take me from my judgement chambers, turncoat!" Pacumení seethed.

"You're right on both counts," Coriantumr said, pulling a silver plasma pistol from her belt and holding it to Pacumení's head. "You *won't* be leaving these chambers; and I *am* a turncoat."

Before the man could respond she fired, sending a high-pitched squeal through the room followed by the smell of burning pork and singed hair.

Pacumení fell to the ground in a lump, a hole the size of a small coin seared between his eyes.

Back stiff, muscles tense, Helaman waited for his turn. Thoughts of his wife and children flittered through his mind along with the wish he had moved from Zarahemla years before.

"I always hated that man," Coriantumr said, looking down at the dead magistrate in his justice robes. "He was always so pompous, as if the fact that his father was Chief Judge somehow made him better than everyone else." She looked back up and stepped in front of Helaman. "Not you though, Helaman. Not you. Your father was even more famous than his; second only to the worshiped Captain Moroni. And yet somehow you avoided turning into a complete self-absorbed waste. How did you do that? If you don't mind my asking."

"Why did you kill everyone on Station Gideon?" Helaman questioned, eyes locked on the shorter woman in front of him.

Coriantumr frowned playfully. "I had to make sure no one tattled that we kidnapped Governor Bethlehem so we could torture the perimeter sensor codes out of him. Otherwise, you would have seen us coming three days ago as we traveled through under-space."

"There were thirty thousand people on that station," Helaman said through grit teeth.

"And there are twelve million on this one," Coriantumr mused, patting Helaman's cheek. "If I had known it would be so easy to overwhelm your defenses, I would have asked King Tubaloth to let me attack your most central and powerful space station sooner. Peace has obviously made your civilization feeble. I thought Moronihah's army would have been better prepared. At this rate I'll have the riches of Bountiful Station in my hands by the end of the week."

"Spare the civilians," Helaman said, thinking of his own family and millions of others. "Zarahemla is not a military instillation. Most of the population are families and noncombatants."

"Don't worry High Priest, I have no plans to slaughter millions of people. This base is worth far too much to the Lamanists as a strategic location, and the people onboard will work to feed my army and pay for my ships. Consider yourselves enslaved."

"People will fight back," Helaman promised.

"Please. Your factions have been at each other's throats for the past year. It was *so* easy to get information on how and when to attack this station. I've been in contact with conspirators, all kinds of nasty killers who want to see this society torn down."

"Men like Kishkumen?" Helaman questioned, hoping to glean more information from Coriantumr if possible.

She looked toward the ceiling as if thinking. "Not familiar with that name. But there are plenty willing to sell information in exchange for favors."

"Captain!" a black and yellow uniformed soldier shouted,

running into the Judgement Hall and waving a rifle over his head. "We've secured this section of the station, but tertiary units are facing resistance in the forward sectors."

"Send a message to Gadianton," Coriantumr replied. "He's supposed to have given us the codes to the shutdowns in that area if we had any problems."

"Who's Gadianton?" Helaman asked. "Only a lower judge would have access to those codes."

Coriantumr ran her tongue across her upper teeth. "I'm sure you'll meet the man soon enough. He's not one to trifle with, I can tell you."

"We're going to fight back, one way or another," Helaman hissed.

"And I'll kill you all as easily as I did your vaulted Chief Judge." Coriantumr turned and spun her finger in the air as if commanding her men to wrap things up. "It looks like the High Priest is bleeding in a couple spots. Patch him up quickly and throw him into one of the holding cells. Then gather the remaining judges and council members. Have we gained control of the central hub yet?"

General Cohor stepped forward. "I just received a report that the barriers are holding, but that we should breach them within the hour. The station has fallen more quickly than we anticipated."

"Good," Coriantumr continued. "I want to do a station-wide broadcast as soon as we have access to the central computers so everyone on Zarahemla knows and understands their occupied status. We must make it clear that they will not be harmed so long as they keep doing their jobs. Gather a few civilians for a public execution just to make sure they know I'm serious."

Helaman pushed against the guards. "You can't kill innocents!"

Turning with a look that could boil water, Coriantumr barred her teeth like a rabid cat. "I can do whatever I want! I would kill you right now if it weren't for the fact that you'd turn into a martyr like that old Abinadi and cause me more problems dead than alive. Take him away."

Soldiers bashed their rifles against Helaman's back, pushing him toward the remains of the towering wooden doors. He tripped on Pacumení's body, stumbling forward toward enslavement and death.

An almost imperceptible vibration moved up his arm from the computer on his wrist. Glancing down quickly, Helaman saw the screen swirl with color and reveal two lines of text: *Priority code Helaman 5-12 received. On the way.*

Helaman smiled. Moronihah had got his message.

Even so, the armada would need time and opportunity if they wanted to repel the Lamanists without destroying Zarahemla. It would take at least two days for Moronihah to arrive from the border. He would need to catch Coriantumr by surprise to avoid a pitched battle around the station that would potentially kill hundreds of thousands. But if Moronihah knew where to ambush the Lamanist fleet just as they took off toward Bountiful, that would give the captain an advantage.

An idea formed in Helaman's mind. If he could get any strategic plans to Moronihah they would have a better chance of sending the invaders scurrying back to King Tubaloth.

Reaching slowly to his computer, Helaman pressed the reply button and held it down to record his next exchange.

"There's no way you'll be able to take Bountiful," Helaman shouted back to Coriantumr as the soldiers thrust him through the door. "Word will reach them of this attack within 24 hours. Their defenses will be at full strength before the week is out."

"Don't you worry about that, High Priest," Coriantumr called. "My main fleet will be on its way once our engines have recharged. Even if the remainder of your forces try to stop us, we'll crush them as easily as we did your defenses here. I have things set so Bountiful will be mine before the morning bells ring on the Sabbath."

"You'll never charge your engines in time," Helaman said, pulling against his escorts to keep the conversation moving. "It will take at least five days before you can make the jump into under-space."

"Not if I piggyback on Zarahemla's solar arrays. In three days, we'll be ready to go. Get him out of here," she said with a wave of her hand.

Helaman pulled his finger from his wrist computer and glanced down to see the 'All broadcast channels are temporarily backlogged with calls' reply. Hopefully, the message would send soon enough to have an impact.

Lamanist soldiers marched through the main hall past Helaman, ushering crying civilians into side buildings and shooting men throwing bottles at the intruders.

"You need to hurry, Moronihah," he whispered to himself. "We're not going to last long on our own."

"The Lamanists aren't staying on Zarahemla," Moronihah said, hands planted firmly against the glass command table in his central war room. Eleven faces reflected in the glass in front of him: generals in military uniforms all stern and resolute.

Commander Jacobs frowned, thick gray beard almost completely hiding his lips. "How do you know this?"

"I received a priority message from Helaman," Moronihah answered. "He recorded part of a conversation with Coriantumr. Her plan is to charge their ships as quickly as possible using Zarahemla's solar array and head directly for Station Bountiful, leaving only enough soldiers on Zarahemla to cow any uprisings."

"This gives us an advantage if we can arrive and attack just as their fleet is preparing to leave," General Abish said, white bangs sweeping across her forehead. "Their weapons won't be prepared to return fire and we can catch them completely off-guard."

"Coriantumr is overconfident," Moronihah continued. "The fact that she was able to sneak past our perimeter defenses and capture our most powerful station has led her to believe our forces are weaker than they actually are. It's clear by her actions that she thinks her fleet will be relatively unopposed. I'm going to send the majority of the armada directly into Zarahemla space. My ship, the Covenant Sword, will lead the attack and bring down Coriantumr's vessel. Shortly after we arrive, I'm ordering Captain Lehi and his ships to jump in from the direction of Bountiful. This will throw the Lamanists off-guard and likely scatter them further. Lehi is the only commander left from the old war and the Lamanists are still terrified of him."

"It's a good strategy," Jacobs said. "Lehi won't give them any room to breathe."

"Can we get anymore messages through to Zarahemla?" Abish questioned. "If we got precise numbers we could attack at the optimum moment."

Moronihah shook his head, sitting down in his seat for the first time since the meeting began. He rubbed his weary eyes, trying not to think about all the people currently enslaved on Zarahemla.

"Communication with Zarahemla has been completely cut off," he said. "But I have some plans in place that could work to our advantage."

"What are you orders, Captain?" Jacobs asked.

"I've already talked to my head of engineering. They're

running numbers to see how quickly the Lamanist fleet can recharge using Zarahemla as a power base. That will at least give us a window for attack. All ships are to prepare for under-space travel within the hour, but our final jump times will be based off what my team comes up with. We don't want to arrive too early or too late."

Abish's wrinkled face turned downward in a worried scowl. "And what of the people on Zarahemla? If all goes well and we're able to repel their armada, the station will still be under Lamanist control. Their soldiers could choose to start slaughtering civilians just as they did on Gideon."

"I'm trusting Helaman in that regard," Moronihah replied. "Just as I'm sure he's trusting us to arrive at the right moment."

"That's a lot of trust," Jacobs said.

Moronihah interlaced his fingers in front of his chest. "Maybe 'faith' would be a better word. We are dealing with the High Priest here, after all; one that has bloodied his fists more than once. Hopefully in three days he'll be ready to drive our enemies into space."

Helaman's cell offered little in the way of comfort beyond a thin mattress and toilet. Limited ventilation blew cold air from above, keeping the prison at a consistently uncomfortable temperature.

Rubbing his hand along the scruff of his three-day beard, Helaman wondered how badly he smelled and wished to feel the warm water of a shower on his face. Or at the very least a change of clothes. Dried blood still covered his sleeve from where he had held Corporal Samuel as he died. The bandage under his left arm could use a changing as well.

His bare feet pressed against the chilly cement floor, sending chills up his legs. A pair of socks would be welcome if nothing else.

The hinged slot at the base of his cell door where the guards slid his meager meals clacked open and then shut. His eyes glanced over quickly, waiting for the flap to open a second time. It moved in his periphery.

The signal had been given.

"Judge Helaman," a mousy voice said.

Helaman scrambled over to the slot, crouching low to the ground. Red hair touched the concrete next to pale fingers with glittery purple nail polish. He couldn't see the face but knew who was risking everything to come speak with him.

"Ruth."

"We only have a couple minutes until the guards return, sir."

"That's enough time. What have you learned?"

Ruth took a deep breath as if about to dive into the ocean. "The Lamanist fleet is setting off toward Bountiful within the next few hours. The guards are going to bring you out to the main plaza stage, where all the music acts perform, along with council members and judges who refuse to work with the Lamanist regime. I heard that after Coriantumr gives a broadcast message from her flagship, all of you will be publicly executed."

"That's what I would expect," Helman said, adjusting his elbows against the hard cement. "They want to get rid of us all at once in one giant display. Moronihah will be here by then. I'm sure of it."

"I hope so. There were apparently whispers of keeping you alive so your death wouldn't inspire a revolt, but one of my contacts said your military history frightened enough of Coriantumr's generals that she conceded to have you killed."

"How's my family?" Helaman asked.

"They're still hiding at my place," the paralegal answered. "Soldiers have been patrolling everywhere, but my apartment hasn't been searched yet. They're safe for now. Isabel is more worried about *you* than anything. Nephi wanted to come here with me, but I knew you wouldn't want him risking something like that."

Helaman reached over and grasped Ruth's hand through the food slot. "Thank you. For everything. Now get out of here before you're caught."

"Yes sir," she said, pulling her hand away and disappearing from view.

Her shoes tapped against the floor and moved quickly down the hall until only silence remained. Helaman sat back up and leaned against the cold wall. Since his wrist computer had been confiscated Helaman had no way of knowing if Moronihah had received his recorded message of Coriantumr's plan.

"Have faith; have faith; have faith," he repeated to himself.

Prayer had been his only solace over the past three days.

After another hour the hinges on his cell door creaked in the silence. Two armed Lamanist guards stomped in and yanked Helaman from his seated position.

"They want you in the plaza, High Priest," one of the soldiers mocked. "Don't worry, you won't be there long."

With a rough shove the soldiers pushed Helaman stumbling into the hallway. Bare toes stubbed against the rough floor, again making the judge wish he had been issued a pair of socks.

"Keep moving," the guard bellowed as they exited the prison level and followed a ramp upward toward the central plaza.

Two teenage girls hurried past as they ascended, doing their best to avoid eye contact with the Lamanist soldiers. No other civilians came into view until Helaman entered the marketplace, where small groups of people huddled nervously next to retail huts full of sunglasses and cheap 'I Love Zarahemla' t-shirts. The local residents looked pale and scared as if waiting for troops to open fire on them at any moment. Gone were the laughing families you would find filling the plaza on a Saturday evening, replaced by frightened refuges forced from their homes to partake in the macabre exhibition.

Scorch marks marred the otherwise pleasant square; broken concrete reminding Helaman of the battles that raged throughout Zarahemla only a few days before. The glass ceiling above looked out on the stars and the Lamanist fleet amassed overhead. Helaman tried to count the ships as he walked past potted plants and small trees, imagining Moronihah appearing in the sky with his armada and laying waste to Coriantumr's flagship.

A forceful shove pushed Helaman closer to the stage where over a dozen of his fellow judges and council members waited for their capital punishment. 25 soldiers stood at the base of the performance area among the tables and chairs of what had been a food court before the invasion. Helaman and Isabel had eaten here once for their anniversary during a live concert.

The context of everything on the station seemed to have changed since the surprise Lamanist attack. Even the most innocuous memories now seemed tainted by the presence of war and blood.

The group of Zarahemla magistrates huddled close together on the theater platform looking as haggard as Helaman felt. Despite the uncertainty of their situation, stiff lips and protestant eyes displayed their firm resolve to not bend to the enslaving force.

A handful of Lamanist soldiers stood on an upper balcony, pointing, and laughing as Helaman walked toward the stage. Their jeers did little to cow the High Priest's determination.

Three television cameras stood on tripods below the elevated arena. Helaman stepped over cables running from inputs on the sides of the video equipment toward receivers next to one of the electronic billboards hanging from the ceiling. Apparently, the execution was going to be *very* public.

Helaman lumbered up the stairs and stood shoulder to shoulder with his colleagues. Looking around at the gathered officials, Helaman couldn't help but notice more than half of the councilmen and magistrates who should have been among the group were missing for unknown reasons. He assumed some of them had been killed while putting up a fight, but also had to admit others likely joined the oppressors to save their own skins.

A quick glance at the crowd confirmed his suspicions as he caught sight of Councilman Antiom standing with several other Zarahemla officials next to a line of Lamanist soldiers. As a being of almost infinite political savvy, it made sense Antiom would sell his soul for whatever scraps he could get.

Helaman stared at the man until they locked eyes. Antiom quickly looked down to avoid the silent confrontation and never raised his head back up, as if his shoes had suddenly become the most fascinating things in the universe.

"What should we do, High Priest?" the delegate to Helaman's right whispered. The judge's name escaped Helaman's mind at the moment, but he remembered meeting him at an official dinner some years before.

"Stand your ground," Helaman answered.

"What if they fire on us? We're unarmed."

"We stand firm no matter what. If we are to die today then we will do so with honor, and hopefully inspire others with our courage."

The man sniffed; mouth turned down in a wounded grimace. "I don't want to die…"

One of the nearby guards caught sight of the tears and turned his rifle on the judge. "Shut up, you! Everybody shut up!"

Fear forced the gathered victims to cluster closer together, squeezing Helaman between the crying judge and four other magistrates and bishops.

The air crackled with the sound of static, followed by a loud screech. The billboards and advertising screens throughout the plaza suddenly lit up with Coriantumr's image, filling Zarahemla with her wicked smile and tattooed forehead.

"Lamanists!" she shouted, voice reverberating unnaturally from each broadcast receiver. "Over the past three days we have prepared for our assault on Bountiful Station, and now in our glory we will rain fire from our armada and reap the treasures of that base!"

Soldiers cheered, noise echoing along the glass surfaces and storefronts.

"Now, to the citizens of Zarahemla," Coriantumr continued. "My soldiers are ordered to execute anyone out of their homes past curfew and anyone gathering in public squares for any reason. To show you how serious I am I will be putting to death a selection of religious and political leaders who have chosen to stand against our new regime."

The image on the screens changed, picking up the signal from the cameras next to the stage. Helaman and the other delegates filled every television and video unit in the plaza; the entirety of Zarahemla likely watched the same broadcast.

Voice-over from Coriantumr continued as the camera panned the group. "These men and women are enemies of the peace and will stand as examples of what happens to those who don't have the greater good at heart."

Switching back to Coriantumr's arrogant face, the broadcast continued. "I am fair, as is King Tubaloth, the Lamanist sovereign...*your* sovereign now. You will be treated well so long as you willingly serve. The men and women about to be executed have proven they would rather put all of you at risk as opposed to work to save you. This group includes…"

Coriantumr paused, looking off-camera as if someone spoke to her about something important. The smug look on her face receded, blood draining from her cheeks.

"How many?" the Lamanist commander asked the unseen individual. After a pause she stepped slightly back from the camera. "That's impossible. When will they break through under-space?"

"What's going on?" a woman whispered from somewhere behind Helaman.

"Get ready," the High Priest said, volume rising. "I think Moronihah is about to arrive."

"Sir! We're dropping out of under-space in three…two…one…"

Moronihah's hands held tight to the armrests of his command chair as the flagship Covenant Sword shuddered wildly. Black nothingness stared at him through the warcraft's primary window before exploding in a psychedelic display of rotating colors.

Under-space travel affected everyone differently. In Moronihah's case, his eyes pulsated with reds, greens, and purples, while the taste of iron and magnesium coated his tongue. Sometimes he would smell his grandma's cookies as well, but this time only the fumes of overheated engines crashed against his olfactory.

Blinking his eyes, Moronihah looked through the glass to see the colors fading, replaced by a massive ring against a field of stars.

Zarahemla.

Next to the space station, less than ten miles distant, sat the

Lamanist fleet ready to set off toward Bountiful. Two hundred ships at least clustered together like ducks in a pond. The lead vessel, large, gray, and shaped like an oval with three lateral engines on both the port and starboard sides, glowed with a halo of white energy in preparation for under-space travel.

Moronihah's timing couldn't have been more perfect.

"Open a channel with the Crimson Descent vessel and all connected ships," he said.

"Done, sir," the communication chief relayed.

"Lamanist fleet," Moronihah began, voice echoing through the speakers throughout the bridge. "This is Captain Moronihah, son of Captain Moroni. You are ordered to stand down or be destroyed. Anyone who surrenders will be spared; anyone who fights will be obliterated. And Coriantumr, I know you can hear this broadcast. Reply with your admission of defeat now, otherwise I will accept your silence as a challenge."

Moronihah waited. No response materialized.

"No signals are coming in from the Lamanists, sir," the communication chief informed.

"Several of the battleships are turning to intercept us, Captain," Lieutenant Jesse said.

"Target enemy cruisers and open fire!" Moronihah ordered. "Send out a fleet-wide command now! All primary vessels converge on their flagship. Re-issue orders to the Lamanists to surrender, otherwise I want Coriantumr burning in space by dinner."

"Yes sir!" Lieutenant Jesse replied from his seat at the helm.

Twenty other officers worked frantically on the bridge, relaying messages, and aiming weapons in preparation for the assault. Moronihah had hand-picked each man and woman on his command team, trusting every single one implicitly. Now they would be put to the ultimate test in the biggest battle any of them would likely experience.

Zarahemla grew large in the window as Lamanist ships began to break formation to head off the newly arrived armada. Flashes of pale yellow lit up the front end of Moronihah's ship as cannons fired into space. Low rumbles echoed from deep in the vessel, ordinance igniting and launching incendiary shells toward the enemy fleet.

Explosions lit up the sky, reflecting in the glass ceiling. Helaman watched in awe as the two armies converged in the stars above Zarahemla.

"Moronihah! That's the Captain's ship!" someone in the crowd shouted.

"The Galactic Navy has arrived!" another chorused.

Helaman looked around at the Lamanist military personnel standing in the plaza. Mere moments before, their faces had gleamed with the confidence of conquerors about to stomp on an enemy's neck. Now they shuffled about, nervous as gazelles in a den of lions.

No better moment will present itself than right now, Helaman thought.

Charging forward, he jumped off the stage and tackled the lead Lamanist official. They hit the ground hard, soldier smacking his nose with a bloody crunch. Helaman ripped the man's rifle from his arms and stood, firing into the collection of distracted soldiers.

"Fight!" Helaman cried. "Fight now! We have them outnumbered!"

He shot three other guards, laying the men out on the stone plaza before any of the soldiers thought to react. Several men from the civilian crowd rushed the Lamanist militiamen as they backed away from the High Priest, wrenching guns from their grasp and joining the revolt.

Enemy soldiers along the second story balcony hurriedly pulled pistols from their belts, but before they could take aim found themselves blitzed from behind by a group of teenage boys. Shocked cries left the infantries' lips as they were pushed over the glass railing and plummeted toward the ground.

Chaos instantly spilled through the plaza like sewer water from a broken pipe.

Councilmen and women leaped off the performance platform and slammed into soldiers preparing to shoot at their enemies. Helaman laid down cover fire as best he could, darting next to the stage to avoid being shot by nearby marksmen. Three lower judges and two bishops fell dead to the floor before they had a chance to pick up a weapon, but soon their bodies were joined by more and more corpses in Lamanist uniforms.

Within minutes the rebels had retaken the square and forced the remaining occupiers to retreat into back hallways and farther down the main marketplace.

"Sound the alarm!" Helaman shouted, pointing toward the balcony. "You boys up there. Watch for any soldiers coming into the plaza and yell if you see any!"

The youth nodded and ran toward an elevated bridge to comply with their orders.

Helaman reached down and picked up a pistol smeared in blood and handed it to one of the councilmen standing next to him. "Everybody else, grab any weapon you see and get ready to continue the fight."

"Judge Helaman!" a tall, bearded man wearing dirty judge's robes called from across the plaza. "A couple of soldiers have barricaded themselves in one of the restaurants and taken hostages!"

Looking around at the ragtag group before him, Helaman knew their victory would be temporary if the rest of Zarahemla's residents refrained from defending their home. He stepped forward, tripping on a tripod that had fallen over in the commotion; a camera still attached to the headpiece.

"Who here knows how to hook one of these cameras up to the broadcast array?" he asked.

"I do," an older woman said, stepping forward with a bloodied pipe in her hand. She wore faded shorts and a tee shirt; an ornate tattoo on her left arm featuring the symbol of the Free Speech Union.

"You're a guild member," Helaman said, crouching to pick up the discarded camera.

"Yeah," the woman replied, tossing her pipe aside with a brash clang. She reached over to help Helaman reposition the tripod. "I handle the filming for all of our meetings."

"Alright, so you can get this hooked up?"

The woman nodded. "We'll be up and running in less than two minutes."

An explosion rattled the square, sending dust and small chunks of plaster falling from the mortar along the glass ceiling. Three military spacecraft shaped like metallic teardrops zoomed dangerously close to the station, firing on each other without regard for the safety of anyone on Zarahemla. One of the ships took a hit and crashed in a brief burst of flame that blackened the windows and threatened to crack open the protective panes.

Startled cries followed the impact's dull rumble. Two councilmen darted beneath a table in the food court as if the flimsy aluminum furniture would protect them from being sucked into space.

"What should we do?" someone shouted from the balcony.

"They're going to destroy the station!" another voice added.

Helaman jumped onto the stage, seeing the space battle intensifying above Zarahemla. "Moronihah is up there right now!" he shouted. "We all need to be ready to fight down here. I'm going to broadcast a statement to get everyone ready to fight. We need to trust that Moronihah will keep us safe. I can guarantee he's counting on us to do what's necessary to liberate the station."

"I don't know how to fight!" a woman cried, waving her hands spastically.

"They'll kill us all!" an overweight man yelled while slamming his fists against a table.

"Put your fear aside and think about everyone else for a second," Helaman urged. "There are way more of us than there are of them at this point. We'll be able---"

"Alright, we're ready to broadcast," the woman behind the camera interrupted. "Save the speech for when everybody can hear it. I've hooked us into the same signal that Lamanist lady was using."

"We're ready?" Helaman asked as his face suddenly flashed on every display screen in the plaza.

The woman waved her hand to draw his attention back to the camera. "You're on!"

"Okay…" Helaman hesitated. Taking a deep breath, he said a silent prayer that the right words would come to his mind. "Citizens of Zarahemla, I am Judge Helaman," he began, voice echoing throughout the marketplace from one end of the ring to the other. "Many of you will also know me as the High Priest of our church. Right now, Captain Moronihah is battling the Lamanist fleet above our heads. Their victory won't mean anything unless all of us down here stand up and fight too. Everyone within the sound of my voice needs to come out in force and help throw the occupiers out of our station. We outnumber them a thousand to one at this point, but we still need every man, woman, and child.

"And to all Lamanists within the sound of my voice: if you surrender now, I can promise that you will be treated well and not harmed in any way. My father and Captain Moroni made this same promise during the war, and it was upheld. I assure you; this pledge will be as well."

Frightened faces in the crowd looked up at Helaman as he spoke. Addressing them directly, he continued. "I know a lot of you are scared on both sides. Don't be. Lamanists, surrender now; citizens of Zarahemla: be prepared to fight for your families just as the Title of Liberty embroidered on our flags prescribes. We all need to show valor and trust in the Lord to strengthen us and lead us to victory. It's time we took back our home! May the God of our Fathers grant us safety and courage. Join me now! Zarahemla is ours!"

A cheer rang out on all sides of the plaza. Helaman nodded to the woman behind the camera, and she ended the broadcast. Stepped down from the stage, Helaman looked on the gathered rebels.

"Alright, break into units of tens. For those who aren't ready to fight, follow those who are and help with the wounded, okay? I don't want anyone who isn't comfortable with a weapon feeling like they have to fight. You don't; but we still need your help."

"Follow Judge Helaman!" a man cried, holding a Lamanist rifle over his head.

Helaman smiled. "Okay everybody, let's get to work!"

"I'm receiving reports of heavy damage to Captain Lehi's ship, sir!" the communication chief yelled over the detonations rocking Moronihah's vessel. "It's unknown how long they'll be able to support us before they lose power."

"Order Lehi to back off," Moronihah said, gold fillings in his molars practically vibrating out of his teeth.

A panel above the main command console exploded, sending sparks raining down on the bridge officers. The smell of smoldering plastic filled the bridge with its pungent formaldehyde stink.

"We've lost lateral thruster 347!" Lieutenant Jesse shouted.

"Keep firing on the advancing cruisers," Moronihah ordered as he watched three jetfighters approach his ship before being destroyed by defense cannons. Rubble slammed into the hull directly in front of the main window, spitting shards of metal and engine parts toward the reinforced glass.

A large ship in the distance, easily twice as big as any of the others, turned its attention toward Moronihah and his crew. The front end came into view, revealing a massive red circle.

"That's Coriantumr's battleship," Moronihah pointed. "Order Generals Jacobs and Abish to bring their fortress-vessels around and flank her position. I want a full press so that they don't have a moment to breathe."

Lieutenant Jesse swiped his fingers furiously across the glass communication screen in front of him, face lit up by changing prompts and alert signals. "Yes sir."

Small jetfighters coursed through the cold vacuum and pelted the Covenant Sword with laser blasts.

"Clear the individual fighters so we can get a clear shot of the Crimson Descent," Moronihah commanded.

Coriantumr's ship fired lateral engines and moved closer to the heart of Moronihah's armada. Mortars lit up the intimidating vessel's front end as shells streaked through space on a collision course with the Zarahemla flagship.

"Captain, the lead vessel has locked onto us and fired exploding ordinance!" one of the gunners informed.

"I can see that!" Moronihah spat. "Evasive maneuvers!"

The ship tilted to the right, forcing Moronihah to hold onto his chair to keep from falling out. Stars swished by outside the window as they veered away from the onslaught, but not fast enough. A jolt cascaded through the ship as at least two of the enemy missiles collided with the reinforced hull. Years of experience in war gave Moronihah a rather good instinct for how his spacecraft would respond to damage. Metal shrieked from deep in the bowels of his ship, followed by a shudder like a dying man with a high fever.

They had taken a direct hit, and if it hadn't broken the back of their vessel, a few more impacts certainly would.

"Return fire!" Moronihah commanded, pulling himself back to a seated position. "Send us on a direct collision course with the Crimson Descent and open every weapons bay we have! I want that ship destroyed now, even if it means we go with her!"

Lieutenant Jesse nodded his head with worried eyes. The Crimson Descent came back into view once more and drew closer as the two ships pointed at each other nose to nose. Cannons exploded in space, leaving behind silent displays of color and flame followed by contrails of smoke. Coriantumr's vessel opened fire as well, turning the black of the cosmos into a kaleidoscope of reds, yellows, oranges, and blues.

Moronihah sat forward as if welcoming the advancing barrage.

Explosions ripped into the hull of both ships sending serrated hunks of steel spiraling into the nothingness of space. Their momentum unimpeded, the crafts continued charging toward each other.

"Sir, we're going to crash into Coriantumr's ship!" Jesse cried.

"No!" Moronihah said, teeth clenched with enough force to shatter bone. "Pivot to starboard now and fire foundation artillery on my mark!"

The Covenant Sword swung to the right at the last second allowing the Crimson Descent to scrape along the vessel's belly. Mortars exploded between the two passing ships, rattling up Moronihah's legs with the force of a jackhammer.

Lights flickered as more sparks rained down from the ceiling and burned against the back of Moronihah's hand. He wiped the searing flakes from his skin and stared out the front window.

"Report!" he yelled, seeing no other ships or jetfighters on the fore.

"Power is fluctuating sir!" the communication officer replied. "I'm trying to reroute communications."

"Turn us about now!"

"Yes sir," Jesse said as sweat dripped from the man's forehead and spattered his command screen.

Gravity pulled Moronihah to the left as the Covenant Sword turned abruptly. Stars streaked like comets outside the window, debris from the battle crashing against the panes.

The Crimson Descent came into view, balls of fire exploding from two of the side engines with breathtaking symmetry. Cavitating to the right, the ship listed like a drunk on a street corner, lights blinking out from one end to the other.

"She's disabled sir," the communication chief informed. "We're still not getting any reports in, but I can tell all six of the port engines are about to go critical."

"We should probably move away," Jesse said without looking back. "With our hull damage we don't want to be near that shockwave."

"Take us back and get communications online," Moronihah

ordered. "We need to know if the rest of the fleet is still fighting or if the Lamanists are going to surrender once their flagship explodes."

"Yes sir."

Sitting back in his chair, Moronihah let out a breath that seemed to take his tension with it. He closed his eyes and prayed none of his generals had fallen during the battle. How had Helaman fared on Zarahemla? Was his friend even still alive?

Moronihah had no way of knowing but would find out one way or another soon enough.

Few details could be seen in the dark restaurant as Helaman poked his head around the corner and peered through the glass. Tables and chairs had been knocked over near the front entrance, but other than that, things seemed quiet.

"They've got three of four people over near the bar," a bearded man with graying hair wearing a leather jacket whispered as he crouched next to the wall. He motioned toward the far end of the establishment with his head. "We ran inside once the fighting started, and most of us made it out when the Lamanists came in, but they captured a few stragglers."

"How many soldiers?" Helaman asked, focusing on a reflection in the mirror behind the bar. Someone stood momentarily before darting back down. That's where the hostages would likely be found.

"Only two."

Helaman looked down at the rifle in his hands. It had been ten years since his last battle during the war; ten years since someone had died at his hands. While he didn't know the exact number,

Helaman estimated he'd killed at least twenty people today. The thought made him suddenly sick to his stomach.

"Alright, we have a few options," Helaman said. "We're going to have to get in and end the stand-off quick, otherwise I'm sure they'll kill the civilians."

"Judge Helaman! Judge Helaman!" a young man in red tennis shoes and a tee-shirt with a sports logo on the front shouted. He ran up to the group of four rebels squatted next to the restaurant entrance.

"Shhhhh!" one of them hissed.

"Shut up, kid!" another urged.

The boy skidded to a halt and kneeled next to Helaman. "Sorry! I was told to come tell you that the central plaza has been cleared across the entire station and that a legion of Lamanists troops have surrendered on the upper ring."

"That's good news," Helaman said, patting the youth on the shoulder. "What's going on outside?"

"The communication channels are crazy right now," the boy answered. "One of my friends said he saw one of the big ships blow up, but he didn't know whether it was ours or theirs."

Helaman turned back to the restaurant. "Okay, go back to where we set up the command center and wait for us there. Understood?"

"Yeah, you got it," the youth said, standing up and running back the way he came.

"Stupid kid could've got those people in there killed," the bearded man spat.

"He didn't know," Helaman defended.

"Well, he better not come over here again or else I'll teach him a thing or two."

"You serve in the war?" Helaman asked.

"Dang right I did. I was in the first battle with Zarahemna, standing next to Captain Moroni himself." the man said proudly, pulling back his sleeve to reveal a faded tattoo with his military unit number.

Helaman drew his face close to the man. "Good for you. Guess what? That kid didn't serve in any war and has never been in a battle before in his life, but still had the courage to help us and come over here to relay a message despite the fact that he knew there were enemy soldiers over here, so cut him some slack."

The man's eyes dropped for a second, lips pressing tightly together. He looked up finally and glanced back through the windows. "So, what's your plan, prophet?"

"To get as few people killed as possible." Helaman stood and handed his rifle to the bearded man. "Take this. I'm not going to need it.

"What do you...?" the man stammered, glancing from the weapon back to Helaman.

"You can't go in unarmed," another rebel protested.

Helaman held his hand forward to silence the group. "Stay here. You'll know if you need to come in guns-blazing."

Opening the door to the eatery, Helaman stepped in slowly. Whimpers echoed from somewhere to his right and he caught movement in the bar mirror's reflection.

"I'm coming in and I'm unarmed," Helaman shouted, walking past a pillar into the restaurant's tavern section.

Tables had been overturned and set up like a makeshift fort on the far end just in front of a cabinet full of various wine vintages. Two heads popped up at the sound of Helaman's voice.

"Stay back or we'll kill them!" a man said, heavy Lamanist accent clinging to his words.

"Hey! It's alright," Helaman replied, raising his hands to shoulder height. "Look, I don't have a gun or anything, okay? I just came to talk."

One of the soldiers jumped up from behind a table and pulled up an elderly woman with him. Gun pressed to her temple, the gray-haired grandma wept, hands shaking uncontrollably. The soldier couldn't have been older than 21, with several facial tattoos around his eyes that Helaman couldn't quite make out in the dark restaurant.

"I'll kill her right now!" the soldier shouted.

Helaman stopped in his tracks. A second Lamanist guard sat up, this one even younger than the first. Dark hair fell over his forehead and almost covered his eyes, which opened wide in apparent apprehension. Two other women, both easily in their 60's and equally as terrified as their threatened companion standing above, peaked over the tables as well.

"Guys," Helaman said calmly. "We don't need to hurt anyone. We can all walk out of here alive."

"You'll shoot us in front of your children," the soldier yelled, pulling the woman closer to him as if needing a shield. "You'll display our bodies in your theaters and parade us around for your pleasure."

"No, we won't," Helaman continued. "I'm Helaman, one of the lower judges here on Zarahemla, and I'm actually the High Priest of our church too. It was definitely before you guys were born, but some of our missionaries came and taught your people. You've heard of Ammon, Aaron, and their brothers, right? A lot of Lamanists came here and joined us in peace. You can too, if you want."

The soldier's eyes narrowed, but he didn't speak. Sweat dripped from his nose.

"Anyway, I'm going to make a promise to you both right now, and you can trust it. Let the women go and surrender. If you do that you can walk out of here with me and I'll send you back to your families. I'll let you go."

The soldier kneeling on the floor behind the table perked up suddenly. "You'll let us go?"

"He won't let us go, Ishmael!" the other Lamanist countered. "He'll have us killed!"

"I won't, I promise." Helaman slowly stepped closer to the men, lowering his hands, and holding them out to his sides. "I swear to you on the honor of my father Helaman, and his father Alma, that I will let you and anyone else who surrenders go free and return to your families."

Pulling his pistol from the woman's head, the soldier pointed it at Helaman. "You're a liar!"

"He swore on the honor of his Fathers, Sherem!" the soldier Ishmael pleaded, looking up at his comrade and the crying woman.

"Your name's Sherem?" Helaman asked, still moving closer. "Sherem, I promise you, and Ishmael here, can walk away from this. If you shoot me though I have a group of soldiers outside that will rush in here, and that will be it for all of us. I don't want to die, and I don't think you do either."

"He swore on his Fathers!" Ishmael repeated, slowly coming to his feet.

Sherem didn't lower the gun. "We're all dead anyway."

"It doesn't have to be that way..." Helaman said.

"Tubaloth will have us all killed for our failure!" Sherem cried, gun shaking in his hand.

"Then you don't have to go back to Tubaloth. You can go and live on Ammon Station if you want. We have a lot of Lamanist refugees living there. You'll be accepted and safe. Just drop your gun and let the woman go."

Face bouncing between rage and confusion, Sherem finally

pushed the woman away and handed his pistol to Ishmael. Helaman stepped over and scooted the toppled tables aside to get to the frightened hostages. The three women embraced him, crying loudly in gratitude.

"Head for the door," Helaman said, pointing over his shoulder. "There are some men out there that will take you to a command center we've set up. Do any of you need medical attention?"

The women shook their heads in unison and rushed toward the exit. A deep breath released from Helaman's lungs as he turned back toward the Lamanist soldiers.

"I'll take the gun," he said to Ishmael, hand reaching for the plasma pistol.

Hesitantly the young man placed the weapon in the High Priest's palm and stepped back as if afraid the man would now shoot him.

Weighing less than two pounds, Helaman looked at the pistol in his hand. Such a small thing and yet with such an immense power to destroy. He wanted to crush it between his fingers and throw it into space, but knew he lacked the power to do either. Instead, he tossed it across the room and listened as it clanged against the tile somewhere on the other side of the restaurant.

"Alright, Sherem, Ishmael, let's go out there and see if anyone has brought some food over to the command post. I'm starving."

"Your men will kill us if we go out there," Sherem protested, stepping back against the bar.

"I promised you would live."

"He promised," Ishmael said.

"You can't make a promise for your men," Sherem countered.

"Yes, I can," Helaman countered.

"How?"

"Because if they try to hurt you, they'll have to kill me first. That good enough for you?"

Sherem blinked several times as if processing the words. Finally, he nodded and followed Helaman toward the door.

"You look terrible," Moronihah said as he led a legion of armed soldiers into the Zarahemla central plaza.

Helaman smiled wearily and stepped forward to hug his friend. "Yeah well, I've been in a prison cell for the past three days and spent the better part of the last twelve hours trying not to get killed."

The friends embraced firmly as soldiers ran around them on their way to fulfill their orders.

Moronihah pulled away and looked around the damaged plaza. "From the reports I've been getting it looks like you guys cleaned up the Lamanists pretty effectively."

"At this point most of them have surrendered," Helaman admitted. "There's a thousand of us for every one of them. Not great odds."

"Still, it could have been a lot worse."

A crash drew Helaman's attention as a group of soldiers threw tables and park benches aside to clear a path for people seeking medical attention.

"It's pretty 'worse' as it is," Helaman continued. "I'm not sure how many civilians have died in the past few days, but easily thousands; maybe even north of ten thousand. The damage is extensive and will take years to repair." He paused, looking upward through the glass and the stars overhead. "Is it wrong I'm just glad my family is safe? Even with all of this, I'm happy I'll get to see my wife and kids in a few hours. So many people are dead, families shattered, and yet I'm happy. It doesn't feel right."

Smacking Helaman on the shoulder, Moronihah smiled. "We take what victories we can get. Don't feel bad about it."

"Don't hurt me!" someone shouted from behind one of the planter boxes and a collection of bushes. "Get your hands off me!"

Helaman recognized the shrill voice.

Two strong soldiers, each easily 6-foot-five, stepped out from behind the plants with Councilman Antiom struggling to pull himself from their grasp.

"We caught this man trying to steal a ship in one of the bays near here," the taller of the two soldiers said, thrusting Antiom toward Helaman. "He claimed to be on official business, but he didn't have proper clearance, and we had a feeling no one had been ordered to leave the station after the attack."

The councilman bowed, hands shaking, eyes wide with terror.

"It's good to see you strong and healthy, Antiom," Helaman said.

"And you, honorable judge Helaman. I hope you understand how I was working for everyone's release and the good of Zarahemla."

A laugh worked its way up from Helaman's stomach at the thought of Antiom doing anything altruistic or remotely courageous.

"I'm sure," Helaman said through the chuckle. "I also hope you'll understand that what I do now is for the good of Zarahemla."

"Judge Helaman..." Antiom stuttered, looking around as if

waiting for someone to rescue him. "I am a powerful man…I have many friends."

"Arrest this powerful man," Helaman said to the guards. "Put him in a nice cold cell with a soft mattress."

"Please!" Antiom screamed, tugging his arms away as the soldiers grabbed him. "I only did what I thought best! I can't be condemned for that! I can't!"

"Bye, Antiom," Helaman said with a wave as soldiers dragged the councilman down the nearest corridor. His shouts echoed long after he'd disappeared around the corner.

"I'm glad I'm not a politician," Moronihah said, wiping sweat from the back of his neck. "At least with people like Coriantumr you know where you stand."

"Is she dead?" Helaman asked.

"Affirmative," Moronihah replied. "Her ship exploded like a firework on New Year's. You guys are going to have thousands of tons of debris to clean up out there in space over the next few months. I have a handful of ships pushing the bigger chunks of wreckage away from the station, but the smaller stuff is already impacting the hull. A few magnet scows should keep things clear before the salvage crews arrive. That reminds me; I've called a council of the remaining magistrates and military leaders so we can come up with a plan for how to proceed with things here on Zarahemla. Some of the other station governors are coming as well."

Helaman raised an eyebrow. "When?"

"The sooner the better. According to your reports this entire station was one bad day away from rioting even before the attack. Things need to get locked down fast so people can go back to their jobs and lives. Pacumení is dead; there needs to be an election; there's a lot of logistics that need to be figured out."

"You're right," Helaman said. "Give us a couple days to get things at least temporarily under control, though. And I need a shower and shave before I can think about any of it."

Chills ran up Helaman's spine as workers scraped metal against stone removing the damaged Judgement Seat from its elevated platform. The screeching bit into his bones until they finally lifted the chair and made their way down the stairs.

The rest of the Judgement Chamber had been cleared of rubble; sections of tile pulled up and replaced with new polished slabs smelling of fresh lacquer. In the two weeks since the Lamanist occupation Helaman had overseen repairs from one end of the station to the other. Time with his family had come at a premium, leaving him lonely and ready to retire from being a judge completely. Moving to Lebanon for some peace and quiet had never sounded more pleasant to him.

A young janitor ran up to the top of the dais and swept away the screws and pieces of concrete left behind by the workers. He nodded and smiled broadly to Helaman, eyes darting quickly away as if he stood in the presence of royalty.

"When will the new seat be installed?" Ruth asked as she walked up to Helaman. Her red hair had been pulled back into a bun; normally colorful blouse replaced by a muted gray pantsuit.

"A few weeks at least," he answered. "The Craftsman's Guild only allowed union members to reopen their doors last Monday, and there's a huge backlog of repairs after the attack. They said it will be a priority, but I'm not pushing them too hard. I always hated that seat anyway."

"Moronihah sent me to find you," she said, tugging on Helaman's arm. "You need to be present for the meeting, and you apparently missed the last one."

"I told you I don't want to be there. You have plenty of leaders already."

"Helaman," Ruth said, pulling the judge to face her. "You know this is important, and *you* are important."

"Yeah, and I'm sick of hearing about it. I want to sit in my living room with my wife and kids and watch a movie or something stupid, not listen to budget debates and delegate stuff anymore."

"If only life were that simple."

Helaman blew out a breath. "I know. Lead the way."

The two friends left the Judgement Chamber and entered the side hallway. Shouts emanated from the main plaza on their left as a construction crew hammered at the concrete to reach a broken water pipe. Shops had reopened along the central ring, returning Zarahemla to some semblance of normalcy.

"A lot of the captured Lamanists have requested to be relocated to Ammon Station,"
Ruth said as they turned away from the plaza toward the council court farther down the hallway. "Some of our transport ships will be taking hundreds out there later this afternoon."

"I hope I'm doing the right thing letting so many former soldiers just go and live on another station," Helaman confessed. "I know it has the potential to come back and bite us."

They approached the double wooden doors leading to the council chambers. Ruth reached for the handle and paused.

"It worked out pretty well when your father and Moroni offered the same mercy during the war. Don't doubt yourself. You're the High Priest. I'm sure God's got your back."

Helaman smiled and stepped forward as she pushed the entry open.

Ruth led Helaman back through the maze of glass hallways toward the private conference room. There 24 men and women sat around a large rectangular wooden table, framed by paintings of former Chief Judges. Helaman scanned the portraits, seeing the image of his grandfather Alma directly behind the chair at the head of the table; a chair that sat empty since the murder of Pacumení.

Looking around the table, Helaman saw no empty chairs waiting for him.

Perhaps they would fire him. The thought cheered his heart a great deal.

"Thank you, Ruth, for bringing our colleague back here," Moronihah said from his seat next to the head chair. "You may continue your duties in the 47th sector, or you can remain here, if you wish."

"Oh, I'm going to stay," Ruth said, bouncing up and down on her heels. "I'll just stand over here along the wall and watch."

Several chuckles emanated from the group as Ruth stepped back toward the wall and stood next to the painting of old Chief Judge Nephihah.

"We wanted to talk to you Helaman," Moronihah continued. "You missed our meeting the day before yesterday."

"And I apologize for that," Helaman said, standing rigid like a child in the principal's office. "I didn't receive word of the meeting until an hour before and I was on the far end of the station ring working with a construction crew who had discovered a gas line rupture near a hospital center. I couldn't leave before all of the details had been worked out to keep the line from exploding."

Moronihah nodded. "It seems you have been instrumental in keeping the peace here on Zarahemla since the attack two weeks ago."

"Your army's presence has helped with that more than a little bit," Helaman said with a playful smirk.

"In any case," Moronihah proceeded. "Your leadership has

been invaluable."

"Thank you, Moronihah, but in fairness there have been thousands of people stepping up to help. Even a handful of Lamanist soldiers have pitched in. It's been a miracle."

"And what of the councilmen who have been arrested?" A magistrate wearing the orange and green robes of Station Mulek asked. "Will they be executed for their crimes against our people?"

"That's up to them," Helaman informed. "Those that give up their positions of power and swear an oath to uphold the freedom of this people will be released, while the others will be dealt with if they continue to act against Zarahemla's interests. I know some of them personally; they won't cause trouble once they're removed from office, I'm fairly sure."

"Understood," the delegate said.

"And what news of the assassins who murdered Pahoran the Second on the Judgement Seat?" Governor Sarah of Bountiful asked. "They must have had something to do with this attack. They had to have been involved somehow. Is there any hope of ever capturing them or at the very least finding out who they were?"

Helaman remembered his exchange with Coriantumr and one of the conspirators she revealed: Gadianton. The name had no meaning beyond her brief mention, but Helaman couldn't help but feel an ominous weight whenever he pondered the man.

"We have a few names is all at this point," he said. "But these men will likely cause more problems in the future, I'm sure, giving us a better understanding of their true motives and numbers."

"What names?" a judge wearing a large magistrate hat with bird feathers along the sides asked.

"Moronihah discovered one of them during his searches prior to the attack on Zarahemla: Kishkumen, who some of you may recognize as the name of one of the Morianton Crime Family's hitmen from back in the day. The other name was told to me by

Coriantumr herself before she threw me in the detainment cells: Gadianton. This one I've never heard of, but the way she talked about him he seems to have at least some influence on this vessel and throughout the country, and a great deal of menace by the way she spoke. I suggest we all begin immediately to seek out any information we can find on these two men and their acolytes."

"That we will, Helaman. Thank you." Moronihah looked up and down the table at the gathered judges, governors, and council members. "There is one further piece of business we would like to discuss."

"And what is that, Captain?" Helaman asked.

"Your name has been submitted as a possible replacement for Pacumeni."

Helaman's neck tightened. "Okay…"

"It was the only name submitted," Governor Sarah added, tapping her finger against the table.

"We'll need to have an election," Helaman said.

"And we will," Moronihah stated. "But we put your name before the guilds and clan heads and all of them will support you. All of them. The people would elect you right now if we sent word for them to start voting."

Helaman walked over and placed his hands on the smooth, reflective table. "I don't want to be Chief Judge."

"I know," Sarah said. "But you're the only name everyone will agree on. If you step back, Zarahemla will be plunged into the same unrest that has threatened the peace since the death of Pahoran the First."

Looking down at his reflection in the varnished wood, Helaman squinted to see any sign of his worthiness to assume the chair once occupied by his grandfather. Alma had been a leader so beloved he cast a shadow from Zarahemla to Bountiful. Helaman could never live up to such a powerful and thoughtful man.

"I'm already High Priest," Helaman countered, grasping for any excuse he could find. "I don't know if I can do all of it and still give my family what they need."

"We're asking a lot," Moronihah conceded. "But if you can think of a better choice, then give it to us now and we'll put them on the ballot."

No names came to Helaman's mind.

What would he do? How could he take on the Judgement Seat without failing everyone in his life?

He said a silent prayer, asking for the right excuse so he wouldn't have to become Chief Judge.

Instead of more justifications however, a peace suddenly washed over him, taking with it his qualms and worries. Zarahemla needed him, and he would be made equal to the task. He would be taken care of, as would his family. In that moment he knew without a doubt.

With renewed faith and fortitude, Helaman looked into the eyes of his colleagues. "Alright, if I'm elected, I'll accept my duty. But before that I'm taking a vacation to Lebanon with my family. Deal?"

"Deal," Moronihah smiled. "Until then though, this council would ask that you take your seat at the head of this table as acting Chief Judge pending such time as the official election can be finalized. We're thinking within a few weeks everything will be certified and the people will have voted. Currently you're a very popular man, so I wouldn't worry too much since it looks as though you'll be running unopposed."

Boots thumped against the cold tiles as Helaman slowly made his way around the group to the empty chair in front of his grandfather's portrait. He paused for a second to look into the eyes of the man he had known as 'grandad,' not 'Honorable Chief Judge.'

Whether or not Helaman could equal the late statesman in judgement or wisdom didn't matter. He would do his best, and that's all God or anyone else could expect from him.

Helaman sat in the chair, soft upholstery conforming to his body like an old couch. He looked down the table at the 24 delegates and their mirror images in the shiny polish as they stared back at him.

"Alright," he said. "Let's get to work."

THE END

Enjoyed *Station Zarahemla*?

Show your support and leave an **Amazon Review**!

OTHER NOVELS BY STEVEN HEUMANN

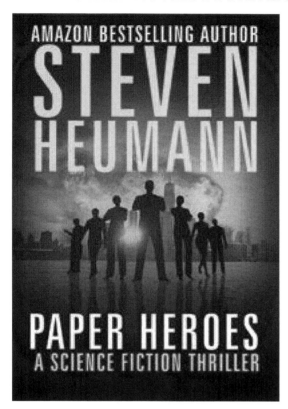

PAPER HEROES:

The bigger the hero, the bigger the lie.

Stewart Mitchell is a nobody, until he witnesses a terrorist attack that changes the world.

Right place right time, or did someone want him in the heat of the explosions?

Who's pulling his strings?

Who wants retribution?

Each choice Stewart makes leads him deeper into a world of fake heroes and villains.

The road to hell? Stewart's paving it as fast as he can. Get ready for superhero thriller where the good guys don't stand a chance. The hunt for Retribution is on!

YOU'LL LOVE PAPER HEROES.

RETOOLED: SCI-FI TALES OF FAIRIES & FOLK

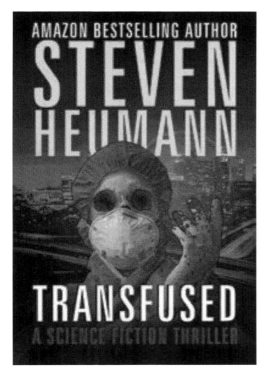

TRANSFUSED

Money. Muscle. Cancer. In the future, they all have one corporation in common.

What if you could receive the benefits of someone else's workout?

That's the promise of TRANSFUSION INC, a trillion-dollar company who offers heath instead of health plans. Anstead Miller is more than happy to get paid to exercise for someone else...until he's pulled into a world of deception, murder, and corporate greed, where even the happiest ending may lead him to an early grave.

TRANSFUSED is a nail-biting sci-fi thriller in the vein of **Andy Weir, Blake Crouch**, and **Michael Crichton**, that tackles the question of what happens when corporate giants start choosing who lives and who dies.

PICK UP YOUR COPY TODAY!

All of Steven Heumann's novels and short stories
are currently available at

www.stevenheumann.com